JUICY AND DELICIOUS

A play

BY LUCY ALIBAR

Diversion Books
A Division of Diversion Publishing Corp.
443 Park Avenue South, Suite 1004
New York, New York 10016

www.DiversionBooks.com

First Diversion Books edition August 2012.

ISBN: 978-1-938120-38-1

Childhood is the kingdom where nobody dies.

—Edna St. Vincent Millay

Quiero hacer contigo lo que la primavera hace con los cerezos.

—Pablo Neruda

"ONCE THERE WAS A HUSHPUPPY"

Several years ago, my wild, brilliant, invincible father started getting sick. Really sick. Prostate cancer led to heart complications, which led to stroke and more heart complications. He lost an eye and had a huge scar across his chest. "Could be checkout time, Boss," Daddy'd say. All of a sudden I felt breathtakingly stupid. I couldn't wrap my head, or my heart, around my parents' mortality. I wrote a play about it, called "Juicy and Delicious", about a frail, cowardly kid in the hot red clay of South Georgia named Hushpuppy, and Hushpuppy's daddy, who was a lot like my Daddy, and Hushpuppy's brilliant and ferocious teacher, Miss Bathsheba, who was a lot like many teachers I've had, and a herd of aurochs. I don't know where the herd of aurochs came from.

We did it at the Tank/Collective Unconscious in Soho, and I had a great time doing it, and then it ended, and I went back to waitressing and writing more plays.

A few months later, I was exhausted and covered in bacon grease from a brunch shift, and I met my friend Benh Zeitlin on the roof of the Russian Turkish baths. Benh and I won a teen playwriting contest when we were 14. If memory serves, his play was about a bunch of vulgar and poetic drunks, and mine was about a Southern Baptist sex-ed class gone horribly wrong. We became friends instantly, and even though he lived in New York while I was in Florida, we'd trade books and mix tapes. He introduced me to Nick Cave; I turned him onto Gram Parsons. I kept writing plays, he made movies. That afternoon on the roof, as he was drinking Czech beer and I had carrot juice, he asked me if I wanted to do my play as a movie, set in Louisiana. I said yes. He pulled out a portfolio of sketches he'd done, pictures he'd taken, and talked to me for I don't know how long about telling Hushpuppy's story in Louisiana, the Aurochs coming from Antarctica, the causeway on the water. Suddenly I forgot that I was tired and smelled like old bacon and burnt coffee and had half-and-half in my hair.

It took us a year and a half to adapt "Juicy and Delicious" into what was, for most of us working on the film, our first—"Beasts of the Sothern Wild". Hushpuppy changed from a little boy to a little girl, because finally I could make the story about a girl. Benh had a long-standing love affair with Louisiana, and after my first week living in a fishing marina outside of Point au Chien, I did too. Have you been there? Sweet Jesus.

The red clay hills of Georgia became the bayou and Gulf. And the confrontation between Hushpuppy and the ferocious aurochs became infused with a grace that it took me several years of working through all of my deepest fears and furies to reach.

This is the play as I wrote it many years ago, covered in bacon grease, raw, angry, and, like Hushpuppy, realizing that there is an order to the whole universe. Even if I am too stupid to see it.

– Lucy Alibar

("Once There Was a Hushpuppy" appears by permission of *Zoetrope: All-Story*)

CRITICAL ACCLAIM FOR *BEASTS OF THE SOUTHERN WILD*

"This movie is a blast of sheer, improbable joy...A lot of thinking has gone into *Beasts of the Southern Wild*, about themes as well as methods, about the significance of the story as well as its shape. And it is certainly rich enough to invite and repay a healthy measure of critical thought."

– The New York Times

"One of the most striking films ever to debut at the Sundance Film Festival, *Beasts of the Southern Wild* is a poetic evocation of an endangered way of life and a surging paean to human resilience and self-reliance."

– Hollywood Reporter

"Brilliant, compelling and powerful, this offbeat look at a part of a world we live in but know nothing about is not going to disappear without at first making a noise."

– NY Observer

"... a stunning debut that finds its dandelion-haired heroine fighting rising tides and fantastic creatures in a mythic battle against modernity....likely to register strongest among critics and cineastes."

– Variety

"The sensation of this year's Sundance Festival, where it won the top award for dramatic (fiction) film and for cinematography, *Beasts* is the odds-on favorite to take the Caméra d'Or prize for best Cannes first feature."

– Time

JUICY AND DELICIOUS CHARACTERS

USHPUPPY: A sweet little Southern boy. Not the sharpest knife in the box.

ADDY: Hushpuppy's daddy. A big, scary Southern man with a glass eye and Georgia Bulldogs hat.

AMMA: Hushpuppy's mamma. She disappeared after Hushpuppy was born, she's just a figment of his imagination. No one else in the play can ever see or ar Mamma except Hushpuppy. When she touches Hushpuppy, it's a "Ghost uch," a few inches above his body. She plays the ukulele.

ISS BATHSHEBA: The School Teacher. She wields a paddle and carries a llwhip.

DY STRONG: A big, scary Southern girl.

IRFDAY CAKE: A Southern Harpo Marx. He's always holding an egg.

UROCHS: Big, scary, extinct bulls, as seen in cave paintings at Lascaux.

NURSE: Played by the actress playing MAMMA.

JAPANESE WOMAN: Played by the actress playing MAMMA.

TRIPPER/WAITRESS.

THE END OF ANATOMY

HUSHPUPPY

"Science: The End of Anatomy. Also Possibly the End of the World."

Hushpuppy picks up a banjo. Plays. It's not good.

While he plays, lights up on a Nurse's office.

The NURSE stands with DADDY , holding an X-ray. She is holding it up to the light. She points at a bad spot. Another. Another. Another.

In Hushpuppy's room, and in the Nurse's office, some grits fall from the sky and fly through the open window.

The three stare at the grits, curious.

A lemon flies in through the window.

Blackout.

DON'T CRY LIKE A BABY

HUSHPUPPY

"Don't Cry Like a Baby."

Hushpuppy and Daddy are in the truck, hunting for dinner. Hushpuppy is crying hysterically.

DADDY

Stupid possum. Stay! Stay there!

(He swerves and misses.)

HUSHPUPPY

Nobody never told me I was gonna die! I don't wanna die! So am I gonna die too?

DADDY

At some point. Don't they teach y'all that at school?

(HUSHPUPPY cries harder.)

HUSHPUPPY

We just learn about manners and how not to look like trash!

DADDY

Well, neither does this here possum, but want want want. DAMN!

He swerves again. Misses.

HUSHPUPPY

I thought only animals die!

Daddy hits a possum. They both cheer up a bit.

DADDY

Hell yeah they do! No more cat food for my Hushpuppy, Boss. Go grab that possum.

HUSHPUPPY gets out of the truck. Retrieves the possum. DADDY watches.

DADDY

Hell yeah. I the Boss Man. I got it under control.

HUSHPUPPY gets back in the truck.

DADDY

Everybody's daddy dies. Mine got ate by wolves. That shit was hardcore. That's how men used to die. My blood's eating itself. You know who dies like that? Cows. My daddy gone by wolves and I gotta die like some milk cow.

Don't cry, Hushpuppy! Makes you look ugly.

Lookit. I'm'll show you a magic trick.

HUSHPUPPY

Magic trick.

DADDY pops out his glass eyeball.

DADDY

Why don't you hang onto it?

3

IT'S THE END OF
THE WORLD, Y'ALL

Hushpuppy at school. A bunch of scrappy kids who are bottom of the food chain.

MISS BATHSHEBA stands before a picture of an AUROCHS.

We hear the sound of ice cracking—a glacier coming loose and falling into the sea.

MISS BATHSHEBA

Welcome to Miss Bathsheba's Finishing School!

Welcome to the End of the World.

A lemon hits the window. Then several more.

MISS BATHSHEBA

Don't pay attention to that. Pay attention to me.
Lesson One: Aurochs.

Long, long ago, when we all lived in caves, the world was swarming with aurochs.

Aurochs were big and hungry and ate babies.

For an aurochs, the perfect breakfast was a sweet, juicy little cave baby. They would gobble cave babies down right in front of their cave parents.

And the cavemen couldn't do nothing about it, because they were too poor, too stupid, too small.

To defy the aurochs would mean a long, painful death.

But even cavemen love their children, in their own, stupid, caveman way; and in their own, stupid, caveman way, they were going to do something about it.

4

e cavemen took whatever weapons they could find— numchucks, or
wtorches, or just their teeth.

ey fell upon the aurochs, screaming, "Toro! Toro! Toro!"

od, and eyeballs, and intestines flew everywhere! And when the war was over,
st of the cavemen lay dead.

t all of the aurochs lay deader.

d now, two million years later, here y'all are.

oof that someone was taking care of you before they even knew you.

cause they loved you with their whole, huge, breaking, stupid little hearts,
en way back then.

he sound of ice cracking. Outside, grits fall from the sky. It's kind of scary.)

MISS BATHSHEBA

on't pay attention to that. Pay attention to me.

ne universe is coming unrendered.

hings are dying ain't supposed to die.

he fabric of the universe is coming all undone.

on't be scairt. Miss Bathsheba's gonna teach y'all how to live through it.

BIRFDAY CAKE'S
SHOW AND TELL

BIRFDAY CAKE stands in front of the classroom, holding his egg.

Music! BIRFDAY CAKE gives us a sweet, stupid little dance, holding onto his egg the entire time.

Birfday Cake shows his class his egg. Bows.

BUILDING A BOAT FOR THE END OF THE WORLD

The kitchen. DADDY's HUSHPUPPY comes home from school. There's nothing in the house to eat but a bag of cat food. He opens the cat food. He eats ravenously.

MAMMA emerges from the bag of cat food. Dripping cat food and flowers. She's fierce, in a Southern-mamma kinda way.

MAMMA

At least eat it off a plate, like a normal person.

HUSHPUPPY puts the cat food on a plate.

HUSHPUPPY

I funna be all alone?

MAMMA

Don't talk with your mouth full! Who raised you?

HUSHPUPPY chews and swallows. Mamma sings and plays banjo.

They sing a stupid fun little jam together, like "Keep on the Sunny Side of Life."

HUSHPUPPY backs her up with some kind of found instrument, like a flour sifter. It's okay if flour gets everywhere. It's okay if it's messy.

DADDY stands in the door, holding a bunch of lumber and some nails.

Some lemons fly through the window.

DADDY picks up the lemons and chucks them back out the window. They fly back in, and he throws them right back.

DADDY

Hushpuppy, who you talking to? You gone retard on me? I swear.

DADDY slams the window shut. Grits and lemons and flowers continue to bombard the windowpane.

DADDY

You funna be OK, even though you too stupid to even use the damn stove. Cause the Boss Man's funna build you a boat. When it's Check Out Time, I funna put you on that boat and you sail to Japan. They don't cook food in Japan. My Hushpuppy's gonna be aright.

DADDY and HUSHPUPPY work on the boat. MAMMA plays the banjo.

The sound of ice melting. A wave soaks the stage. Catfish are washed onto the stage and flop around.

DADDY

Could you touch me?

I can't remember the last time someone touched me that wasn't them trying to stop me from knocking their teeth out or setting them on fire.

HUSHPUPPY hesitates. He doesn't know how to touch people. HUSHPUPPY punches DADDY in the arm, hard.

DADDY

That's good.

You're such a sweet, stupid little booger.

They work on the boat.

Grits rain down outside. A flower falls from the sky.

BAD GIRLS GETTING SPANKED

Lunchtime. HUSHPUPPY is eating from a bag of cat food.

JOY comes thundering up.

JOY

STUPID LITTLE FLAT-FACED PUSSY BITCH DIE DIE DIE DIE DIE
DIE DIE.

JOY snatches HUSHPUPPY's lunch and sets it on fire.

JOY snatches DADDY's glass eyeball from HUSHPUPPY's neck and pockets it.

*MISS BATHSHEBA charges in, whaps JOY with the paddle, and throws herself
on top of HUSHPUPPY's lunch like a Navy SEAL, to put the fire out.*

MISS BATHSHEBA

I swear to God, Joy Strong, sometimes I think you bad on purpose just because
you like getting spanked.

Awright, Hushpuppy. Lesson five—you got to learn to take your own justice.

MISS BATHSHEBA pulls a paddle from her belt and gives it to HUSHPUPPY.

*HUSHPUPPY takes the paddle. Stares at JOY. The lights turn violet. Now we're
in HUSHPUPPY's imagination.*

A flower falls from the sky.

*He whaps JOY with the paddle. Again. Again. He punches JOY in the mouth.
The lights change back to normal.*

JOY

(*To HUSHPUPPY*) Pussy-bitch.

The lights go violet. A flower falls from the sky.

HUSHPUPPY whaps JOY with the paddle. Again. Again. He kisses JOY ravenously.

Her mouth, her neck, her breasts.

The lights change back to normal.

JOY

Stupid little flat-faced pussy-bitch.

The lights go violet. A flower falls from the sky.

HUSHPUPPY whaps JOY with the paddle. Again. Again. HUSHPUPPY screams like a caveman, grabs JOY's head, and sucks out her eyeballs.

The lights change back to normal.

JOY

He a stupid little flat-faced pussy bitch on *food stamps*. He got *head lice*. He eat *cat food*. Yeah I set his lunch on fire. Maybe tomorrow it'll be him.

HUSHPUPPY hands the paddle back to MISS BATHSHEBA.

MISS BATHSHEBA, disgusted, hands JOY the paddle. JOY whaps HUSHPUPPY, hard.

MISS BATHSHEBA

I like your balls, little girl. You gonna survive. Here.

MISS BATHSHEBA gives JOY a cookie. JOY eats it in front of Hushpuppy. She doesn't share.

KEEP FAR, FAR AWAY FROM JOY

JOY

cial Studies: Keep far, far away from Joy.

a river, outside of HUSHPUPPY's house. HUSHPUPPY's boat is partially sembled and tied to the house.

he boat has a sail. A spyglass.

USHPUPPY is sitting on the shore. He's been beaten up real bad. His face is oody.

Y enters, breathing hard. She's run all the way from school.

e's holding DADDY's glass eyeball in her hand.

e and HUSHPUPPY stare at one another.

JOY

ow many teeth did I break?

HUSHPUPPY

hree.

JOY

et you can't eat cat food for a while, huh? Don't you wanna hit me?

he hands HUSHPUPPY back the glass eyeball and steps onto the boat.

HUSHPUPPY

I thought you was gonna burn it.

JOY

I wanna be a sweetheart. I want people to say, "Oh, Joy Strong. She a sweethear

HUSHPUPPY

This here's—

My daddy's building me a boat. For when he—

For when it's the end of the world and we graduate.

I'm supposed to sail to Japan.

I think I'm gonna die when he dies.

I can't swim. And I can't understand Japanese. I can't hardly understand Englis

They stand in the boat. They stare at each other a long time.

JOY

I got all this stuff! Look!

My grandaddy says the Apocalypse is coming! So he gave me all these present
Look!

A blow-torcher! Look!

JOY pulls a blowtorch from her pockets.

Look!

A HUGE knife.

Look!

12

JOY pulls out a lemon wedge and holds it to HUSHPUPPY's lips. Rubs gently.

JOY

My mamma sends me fruit from where she done ran off to. My grandaddy burns the packages she send 'cause he says eatin' presents from my mamma might turn me lesbian.

But sometimes I can sneak 'em before he burns 'em. Relax your mouth. Yeah.

I got a congenital heart murmur. My granddaddy says other people's hearts play white-people music, but my heart plays black-people music. Feel.

JOY presses HUSHPUPPY's hand to her chest.

JOY

My heart's got too much blood in it. At night I feel my heart wanting to explode. So I nail my mind to good things. This'll be what I nail my mind to tonight. All this stuff.

Water. My blowtorcher. A boat somebody made you. Thank you.

JOY puts the rest of the lemon wedge in HUSHPUPPY's mouth.

JOY

My granddaddy says your mamma's a stripper in Marietta.

JOY punches HUSHPUPPY and runs off.

MAMMA appears out of the lake. Drenched.

She climbs onto the boat and strokes HUSHPUPPY's hair.

HUSHPUPPY

I think you work somewhere in a restaurant. You make everything yourself. Your food's so good it's magic. You a magic cook.

MAMMA

Good boy.

HUSHPUPPY

Yes ma'am.

MAMMA

People tell you, when you're a stupid little kid, that your life is gonna be a big, juicy banquet. And they're right. What they don't tell you is sometimes at that big, juicy banquet you're just a stupid little waitress. You carry around a platter with all your organs on it. You offer your organs to people, and either they want them because they're juicy and delicious, or they don't. The polite thing to say is, "No thank you."

But sometimes you offer to people, and they throw 'em to the floor. Make a big scene. Bein' all, "Your organs is nasty-lookin'." "Your organs is bad for me." "Your organs is too rich and they fixin' to *kill* me with their juicy goodness."

Ain't nothing wrong with your organs, Hushpuppy. Some people just got bad table manners.

HUSHPUPPY

Could you touch me?

MAMMA

No. Sorry. Work on your boat.

14

HUSHPUPPY

Yes, ma'am.

MAMMA

Good boy.

GRACE

MAMMA

Grace.

The kitchen.

DADDY is working on the boat.

HUSHPUPPY is eating possum from a bowl.

DADDY

Afterwards. I don't want no service. No Jesus, hear? I don't got time for none of that.

HUSHPUPPY

You don't even want me to say grace?

DADDY

You're in Special Ed. You can't even work the stove. You can't say grace.

HUSHPUPPY

I know how to say grace.

DADDY

You can't even build a boat by yourself.

HUSHPUPPY

can say grace.

DADDY

ou don't even know where Japan is.

HUSHPUPPY

EAR GOD,

HIS IS POSSUM!

OU MADE IT!

OU PUT IT IN THE FIELD!

OU MADE IT STUPID ENOUGH FOR MY DADDY TO RUN IT OVER
ITH HIS JOHN DEERE!

OW IT'S IN MY BOWL!

ND IT'S GOOD!

LIKE IT!

THANK YOU!

Pause)

DADDY

men.

HUSHPUPPY

men.

Some grits fall from the sky.

An egg rolls across the stage.

                    HUSHPUPPY

Make it quit!

                    DADDY

You know. End of the world and all that.

Some lemons roll across the stage. HUSHPUPPY freaks out.

                    DADDY

Hush up, Hushpuppy. Bad for my heart.

A lemon flies across the stage and hits HUSHPUPPY in the head. More freakin
out.

                    DADDY

Hey, boss. I'm'll show you a magic trick.

                    HUSHPUPPY

Magic trick.

DADDY grabs HUSHPUPPY around the waist.

                    DADDY

Jump.

HUSHPUPPY jumps. DADDY lifts him high in the air above his head.

A moment of perfect suspension.

18

MERCY

The classroom. The children are alone, without MISS BATHSHEBA. HUSHPUPPY is eating leftover possum, with hot sauce.

JOY is pouring lighter fluid all over BIRFDAY CAKE. HUSHPUPPY watches.

HUSHPUPPY

Today is different from all the other days because now I have real lunch for lunch, so Joy's gotta find something else to set on fire.

JOY

You ain't too smart, are you?

Lord! You got this sweet little stupid snapdragon face! Lord!

JOY pulls out her blowtorch.

JOY

DON'T YOU UNDERSTAND? SOMETHING COULD HAPPEN TO YOU!

YOU'RE SUPPOSED TO HAVE SOMEONE TAKING CARE OF YOU RIGHT NOW!

AND THERE'S NO ONE TAKING CARE OF YOU!

MISS BATHSHEBA bursts in. She and JOY see each other. JOY freezes.

JOY puts the blowtorch down.

MISS BATHSHEBA strips BIRFDAY CAKE's clothes down to his underwear.

19

Water, soap.

With their hands, MISS BATHSHEBA and HUSHPUPPY scrub lighter fluid off him.

MISS BATHSHEBA

You too, Joy.

Pay attention. This here's the most important thing I'll ever teach y'all.

Quick little circles. Good for the heart. You got to take care of people who are stupider and sweeter than you.

JOY goes to BIRFDAY CAKE. Touches his heart. Gasps.

GRITS AND GATOR

HUSHPUPPY and DADDY are on the partially finished boat.

DADDY is teaching HUSHPUPPY to play the banjo.

We hear an aurochs banging against the door; running into it again, again, again.

DADDY

The melody, Boss, listen for the melody!

Boss did I ever tell you where you come from?

Boss your mamma was so pretty she'd never have to use a stove. She'd walk into a room and all the water would start boiling. Boss when we first met each other, we was so shy we'd just sit around and smile at each other like a bunch of retards. One day I was feeling so shy I had to just lay down and take a nap. I wake up to hear heavy breathing. There's a big ole gator crawled right into the yard, close to me as you are now. Doing that slutty gator breathing. Next thing I know your mamma steps out with a shotgun, just in her little cotton panties, and BAM. She turns around, covered in blood, gives me this big ole smile, and you popped into the world maybe four minutes later. Afterwards we's laying in bed, smiling like a bunch of retards, and I feel like my hearts fixin' to bust outta my chest, and I feel like I do fit, after all, into the whole galaxy. That there's a right good pattern to the whole wide universe and I'm one of them numbers in it. And your mamma sees it too. And right then, grits started falling from the sky. Wsshh. It shoulda been scary but it felt real peaceful. From the sky, through the holes in the roof, into the pots of water on the stove that were already boiling cause your mamma was so pretty. We had grits and gator for days. Your mamma would open cold beer with her teeth. So it's not your fault you can't use a stove, it's a side effect of you being champion of the world.

(HUSHPUPPY plays some more. The aurochs crashes at the door. They jam

21

together. The banjo jams starts to jam stronger and stronger against the roar of the wild animals outside. Now HUSHPUPPY sounds real real good.)

A big chunk of the ceiling falls down. Grits and flowers rain down through the hole in the ceiling. DADDY and HUSHPUPPY are too elated to notice.

DADDY

You the MAN Hushpuppy! You the Man and I'm the Boss Man!

More banging on the door. DADDY opens the door and head-butts the charging AUROCHS. He knocks it senseless and slams the door.

BIG GAY DANCE NUMBER

e kitchen. Nighttime. HUSHPUPPY and DADDY are asleep, in front of the
at.

demon hits DADDY in the head. He wakes up. He sees MAMMA.

DADDY

ey.

MAMMA

ey.

DADDY

u always here?

MAMMA

f course.

DADDY

Iuh.

ou look good.

uck good. You look—

MAMMA

hhhhhhh.

Some flowers fall from the sky. DADDY strokes MAMMA's hair. We hear mus
"Eternal Flame," *a mighty jam.*

MAMMA

Look.

(re: HUSHPUPPY sleeping, peacefully. Breathing in and out.)

Look.

(MAMMA pulls a lemon from her hair. Cuts it. Runs it across DADDY's lips.)

MAMMA

Look. This is how it is, right before the end. Your senses wake up. You see a
these good things that were here for you, all along, and you didn't even know
You hear the heartbeat of God.

DADDY

Is this the heartbeat of God? It sounds gay.

DADDY and MAMMA dance. A herd of AUROCHS dances around them. Th
music swells. Now it's a really big gay dance number.

An AUROCHS picks up HUSHPUPPY and begins to carry him to the boat.

DADDY

Not yet.

DADDY snatches HUSHPUPPY from the AUROCHS. HUSHPUPPY
wakes up.

DADDY lies down close to HUSHPUPPY. He presses HUSHPUPPY's head to
his chest

HUSHPUPPY

When you die I funna die too. When I'm laying in bed at night I start shaking and I can't stop. I feel like I'm coming unlodged. I got what you got.

DADDY

You? Naw. You funna live a hundred years. More, probly.

DADDY holds up his arms in a challenge to arm wrestle.

DADDY

Come on, Hushpuppy, show me them guns. GUNSGUNSGUNS-GUNSGUNSGUNSGUNS.

HUSHPUPPY flexes his arms and shows DADDY his muscles.

DADDY

YEAH BOSS!

DADDY and HUSHPUPPY arm wrestle. DADDY lets HUSHPUPPY win.

DADDY

You the man, Hushpuppy. Who the man?

HUSHPUPPY

I the man!

DADDY

Tell me who the man?

HUSHPUPPY

I the man!

DADDY

That's right you the man! You my man!

DADDY punches a hole in the wall.

DADDY

No cryin'. You king of the dinosaurs Hushpuppy.

Listen for my heart. Make sure it don't stop.

DADDY falls asleep. HUSHPUPPY is wide awake.

HOLDING THE EGG

The Classroom.

HUSHPUPPY stands alone. All of a sudden he can't breathe. He doubles over.

BIRFDAY CAKE tiptoes in, holding his egg. He watches HUSHPUPPY.

BIRFDAY CAKE goes to HUSHPUPPY. Hands him his egg.

They hold it together.

HUSHPUPPY

That's good.

BIRFDAY CAKE nods in agreement.

JOY comes in. Sees them. Goes to them.

The three children hold the egg together.

HUSHPUPPY GOES TO MARIETTA

HUSHPUPPY

It's all getting to be too big for me. The end of the world and the end of math and all that nonsense about my daddy's heart. I am running, running, running. Past aurochs and dragons wrestling on the highway. The swamps are being sucked up into the sky, in green whirlpools, because gravity's broken, too. I bet that's how come I can run so fast.

The air is thick with cicadas. All the trees are on fire. Burning gardenias float through the air like fireflies.

I don't know where I'm going until I get there, but sure enough, I get to Pretty Baby's Gator Shack all the way in Marietta.

HUSHPUPPY reaches the Gator Shack. He's covered in burned magnolia blossoms, cicada shells, swamp grass, and dirt.

Sees the STRIPPER/WAITRESS.

He's pretty sure it's his mom.

STRIPPER

You know whatchu want?

Menu's right here.

HUSHPUPPY can't read.

HUSHPUPPY

I got this much.

He gives the STRIPPER money.

STRIPPER

u ain't too smart, are you?

HUSHPUPPY

, ma'am.

STRIPPER

ouldn't you be in school?

ho's takin' care of you? There should be someone takin' care of you. Lord!
u're just out here all by yourself! So little and stupid! You got this sweet little
pid snapdragon face! Lord! DON'T YOU UNDERSTAND? SOMETHING
OULD HAPPEN TO YOU! YOU'RE SUPPOSED TO HAVE SOMEONE
KING CARE OF YOU RIGHT NOW AND THERE'S NO ONE TAKING
ARE OF YOU!

HUSHPUPPY

s, ma'am.

STRIPPER

ELL IT AIN'T SUPPOSED TO BE LIKE THIS!

HUSHPUPPY

y mamma tore off when I was a baby for reasons unknown, and I don't know
she's dead or a stripper in Marietta, but I have all these ladies bumping into my
fe from every corner of the universe and I wonder if they're her. Taking care of
e from far away.

ou got grits and gator?

he STRIPPER leaves. Returns with a bowl of grits and gator and a bottle of beer.

STRIPPER

Look here. I'm'll show you a magic trick.

The STRIPPER opens the beer bottle with her teeth. Then she cracks an egg ov
the grits.

Squeezes lemon over HUSHPUPPY's egg and grits.

She feeds HUSHPUPPY grits and sings. Just for HUSHPUPPY.

Flowers rain down from her hair and bikini. HUSHPUPPY stuffs dollar bills
her bikini. This should be very sweet and tender.

STRIPPER

(Singing)

You're good! You make me happy!

You're good! You make me happy!

HUSHPUPPY

Can you touch me?

STRIPPER

No. Sorry.

HUSHPUPPY

Yes, ma'am.

STRIPPER

And don't talk with your mouth full.

HUSHPUPPY'S SHOW AND TELL

HUSHPUPPY

Show and tell. By Hushpuppy.

HUSHPUPPY looks at the audience. Takes them in.

Picks up a banjo.

HUSHPUPPY does a stupid little dance. Accompanies himself on the banjo.

He is interrupted by the roar of ice cracking. Water floods the stage. Catfish flop around everywhere. Bubbles fill the air and grits and flowers rain from the sky.

AUROCHS start to run across the stage.

MISS BATHSHEBA, in a rain slicker and water wings, charges onto the stage. Grabs HUSHPUPPY and throws him over her shoulder.

She chucks a lemon at one of the AUROCHS and runs off, carrying HUSHPUPPY.

Things start to fall apart. Big time.

THIS IS IT

The classroom. Moments later.

MISS BATHSHEBA, JOY, HUSHPUPPY, and BIRFDAY CAKE have barricaded themselves in.

We hear all kinds of apocalyptic noises. AUROCHS pawing at the door.

MISS BATHSHEBA

Pay attention! It's the end of the world. Here's y'all's last lesson.

Imagine: I'm trapped in Georgia after a quantum physical Holocaust. Surrounded by beasts of the Southern Wild. All I got for my last meal is one bottle of beer, and it's warm. Then—grace in the wilderness. An icebox. I open the door. I put the beer in the icebox. Now. How long I gotta wait—surrounded by a million animals that want to eat me, 'bout to DIE—how long I gotta wait before I can grab that beer outta the icebox, pop it open with my teeth, and it'll be delicious. Fuck *good*. Delicious. How long?

HUSHPUPPY

Two hours.

(MISS BATHSHEBA whaps him with her paddle. BIRFDAY CAKE holds up three fingers. MISS BATHSHEBA whaps him with her paddle)

JOY

Eleven minutes.

MISS BATHSHEBA

Good Girl! You gonna survive!

MISS BATHSHEBA gives JOY a lemon.

The sounds of wild animals howling at the door are overwhelming.

MISS BATHSHEBA

Pay attention! It's the end of the world.

There's all this stuff.

Apocalypse. Mercy. Aurochs. Grace.

It's the end of the world,

And there are presents flying at you from every corner of the universe. Look. Pay attention.

MISS BATHSHEBA pulls out a bucket from behind her desk. The bucket is filled with weapons—lemons, eggs, grits, and flowers. It also contains three beers, which she opens with her teeth.

MISS BATHSHEBA

I'm'll defend y'all. Now none of y'all can say, "Nobody never took care of me." Miss Bathsheba took care of y'all.

She hands the children weapons. Kisses them good-bye.

MISS BATHSHEBA

Toro! Toro! Toro!

MISS BATHSHEBA charges out, cracking her whip. The sound of the wild animals get louder. They are banging against the window.

The next sequence is a frenzied ninja ballet.

The children defend themselves against the advancing wild animals.

BIRFDAY CAKE is a skilled ninja.

JOY grabs HUSHPUPPY and they retreat farther into the classroom.

HUSHPUPPY touches JOY's hair. Again. Again. Again.

JOY

Look!

Gently at first, then with gusto, beautiful Southern love-tokens fall from the sky: Grits!

JOY

Look!

Flowers!

JOY

Look!

They touch fingertips.

HUSHPUPPY puts his head to JOY's chest.

We hear a huge, beating heart.

Eggs, hundreds of them, roll across the floor from all directions!

Lemons, hundreds of them, roll across the floor from all directions!

Yes! Yes! Yes! Yes!

The music swells!!!!

MISS BATHSHEBA *enters, covered in blood. Dying. The arm that held her bullwhip has been bitten off. Her intestines are hanging out. She's missing an eye.*

MISS BATHSHEBA

The beasts got me! So get! Y'all's graduated.

Be sweet. Take care of each other. And don't never, NEVER be ashamed to look like a stupid little cry-baby bitch. You're gonna look like a stupid little cry-baby bitch most of your life, anyway, if you live a life that's any good. Fuck good. Delicious.

An AUROCHS bursts through the window and leaps onstage. MISS BATHSHEBA leaps into its arms.

MISS BATHSHEBA

Toro! Toro! Toro!

The AUROCHS carries MISS BATHSHEBA off.

MAMMA glides in.

MAMMA

Hushpuppy! You need to go home. Say good-bye to your daddy. It's the End of the World.

MAMMA glides off. The children stand still.

HUSHPUPPY goes to BIRFDAY CAKE. Snatches his egg. He smashes it into BIRFDAY CAKE's head, then climbs out the window.

BIRFDAY CAKE crumbles. JOY catches BIRFDAY CAKE in her arms.

THE END OF THE WORLD

HUSHPUPPY

The end of the world. By Hushpuppy.

HUSHPUPPY's house.

HUSHPUPPY walks into the house. Drenched. Outside we hear the rush *many waters.*

The boat is gone.

MAMMA is sitting on the counter, strumming a banjo. DADDY is slaving ove *a stove.*

DADDY

Hushpuppy! I made you hushpuppies, Hushpuppy! Your boat's out front.

HUSHPUPPY

Nuh-uh.

DADDY

Yes-huh.

DADDY takes out three eggs. DADDY cracks and beats the eggs into a bow *While he talks, he makes hushpuppies and puts them into a lunchbox, along wit* *flowers, eggs, grits, and lemons.*

DADDY

When you was born, we were both so scared we'd accidentally break you or leav
36

you in the icebox or something. So your mamma stayed awake with you all the time, wouldn't cook no more. All I knew how to make was hushpuppies and grits, so that's what we ate for a week.

MAMMA

And we couldn't think of a name.

MAMMA and DADDY

We just called you Big Fat Baby.

DADDY

You didn't make any noise. So sweet. The three of us would sit, eatin', lookin' at each other. One night your mamma says,

MAMMA

"We call him Hushpuppy. A Hushpuppy is a—

DADDY

small,

MAMMA

stupid,

DADDY

warm,

MAMMA and DADDY

—good little thing."

37

The three of them sit on the counter and eat hushpuppies.

DADDY

But I did good, right? I raised you and you didn't die. You don't got worms. Anymore.

You ain't in the Klan.

So already I done a better job than mosta the daddies in this town.

I mean hell, people give you something to take care of, mosta time you end up breaking it, or losing it or settin' it on fire, and you will too, so ease up, Boss.

DADDY hands HUSHPUPPY a lunchbox full of hushpuppies, flowers, grits, eggs, and lemons.

DADDY

You're good, Hushpuppy. You make me happy. Don't bang the door and act like a little cry-baby trying to get back in.

DADDY scoops HUSHPUPPY up in his arms. DADDY carries HUSHPUPPY to the door. MAMMA opens it.

Outside is a great flood. The boat is tied up to the porch. DADDY puts HUSHPUPPY on the boat. He shuts the door.

HUSHPUPPY doesn't make a sound.

LUCY ALIBAR

MIDNIGHT ON THE OCEAN

HUSHPUPPY, in his boat, in the sea. He is holding up DADDY's glass eyeball, against the night sky. A billion stars are reflected in the water.

HUSHPUPPY

When I relax behind my eyes I can see all the molecules of the universe. And the measurements and equations behind all of it. When I look too hard it goes away. But when I breathe in and let the universe reveal itself unto me, without me trynna change it, I see that I am an integer in a great astronomical equation. That I play a part in all of this very, very advanced placement math. And this is a great comfort to me. This knowledge that there is an order, even if I am too much a stupid little pussy bitch to see it.

EPILOGUE:
HUSHPUPPY GOES TO JAPAN.
BIRFDAY CAKE GETS A BATH.

Early morning.

We hear water.

Split Stage:

On one side, the classroom. BIRFDAY CAKE is in a basin filled with water. JOY is giving him a bath. There are soap bubbles everywhere. She pours water over his head. She uses a whole lemon to scrub his body. The hand BIRFDAY CAKE used to hold his egg is now clutching tightly onto JOY's hand.

On the other side of the stage, HUSHPUPPY is on his boat, floating down a river in Japan.

He's got DADDY's glass eyeball around his neck, tied to a string.

A JAPANESE WOMAN on another boat bumps into him.

They both open their lunch boxes.

The JAPANESE WOMAN pulls an egg out of her lunchbox. She cracks the egg into a bowl and beats it with chopsticks. She pulls a bowl of rice out of her lunchbox.

She pours the egg over the rice.

HUSHPUPPY has hushpuppies and grits.

JAPANESE WOMAN

(re: *HUSHPUPPY's breakfast*)

Nan desu ka?

HUSHPUPPY

ıshpuppies. Grits. It's real good.

*USHPUPPY offers the JAPANESE WOMAN a hushpuppy. She takes a bite. She
lls out a knife and a lemon. Cuts the lemon. Squeezes it over the hushpuppies.
elps herself to another one.*

*Y pulls out a huge butcher knife. She cuts the lemon and squeezes the juice onto
'RFDAY CAKE; into BIRFDAY CAKE's bath water.*

JOY

nis is real good for your heart.

JAPANESE WOMAN

shi desu!

HUSHPUPPY

know.

*hey eat together. JOY pours water over BIRFDAY CAKE and scrubs him. It's so
od they don't need to say anything.*

The End.

Inspired by the play *Juicy & Delicious* by Lucy Alibar, award-winning film BEASTS of the SOUTHERN WILD tells the story of a forgotten but defiant bayou community cut off from the rest of the world by a sprawling levee.

Buoyed by her childish optimism and extraordinary imagination, she believes that the natural world is in balance with the universe until a fierce storm changes her reality. Desperate to repair the structure of her world in order to save her ailing father and sinking home, this tiny hero must learn to survive unstoppable catastrophes of epic proportions.

For more information on BEASTS of the SOUTHERN WILD visit www.welcometothebathtub.com.

CAMÉRA D'OR
FESTIVAL DE CANNES

WINNER
GRAND JURY PRIZE
SUNDANCE
FILM FESTIVAL

CPSIA information can be obtained
at www.ICGtesting.com
Printed in the USA
LVHW041713051021
699579LV00005B/84